For an old farm in New Hampshire that waited—
and for every house, waiting
MLR

For a house in Vermont, and all those who lived there
EBG

Text copyright © 2021 by Mary Lyn Ray
Illustrations copyright © 2021 by E. B. Goodale

First edition 2021

Library of Congress Catalog Card Number pending
ISBN 978-1-5362-0097-3

TLF 26 25 24 23 22 21
10 9 8 7 6 5 4 3 2 1

Printed in Dongguan, Guangdong, China

This book was typeset in Usherwood.
The illustrations were done using monoprinting, ink,
watercolor, and digital collage.

Candlewick Press
99 Dover Street
Somerville, Massachusetts 02144

www.candlewick.com

THE HOUSE OF GRASS AND SKY

Mary Lyn Ray

illustrated by E. B. Goodale

CANDLEWICK PRESS

Once, out in the country, someone knew right where to build a house.

Inside it smelled of sunshine and new lumber. Outside smelled of meadow grass and sky.

The house had a tree with a swing,
a garden with roses, and a family.
It was happy.

As years went by, other families came and went.

The house learned about babies being born and babies growing up.
It learned about bedtime stories and birthday parties.

And if it had to learn *Goodbye,* it also learned *Hello.*

Because a new family always came—until one didn't.

Then everything felt different.

The house especially missed the children busy with their games and secrets—
except sometimes, it remembered, the children just sat very still, to think.
The way the house was thinking. It knew a family would come.

And one did. But they said, "Who could live in such a small house?
We'd have to add on."

The house didn't want to be Added Onto. But that family didn't stay.

So the house waited as summer's leaves turned orange and red,
then fluttered to the ground like bright flocks of birds,
while it imagined children running and twirling among them.

Soon cold winter followed. But in the snow and shiver, when everywhere was white, the house remembered roses.

And when spring woke, the roses woke, too. All outdoors smelled pink.

The house welcomed back the green time and every green smell, too. Though some days it also wished for the kitchen smells that it remembered.

Especially the smell of a birthday cake baking.

So when another family came looking,
the house hoped as hard as it could hope
for what used to be.

But that family said "It is too quiet" and went back to the city.

The house liked the country quiet.

It could hear the smallest sounds—of rabbits whispering and buds unfolding.

But it missed the noises children made. And, most of all, it missed the children.

Now, when days turn to dusk, the house is dark.
There is no lamplight at its windows.

But the moon still visits often.
The house knows the moon, the moon knows the house.
They are old friends.

Yet the house can't help remembering when children stood in
rugs of moonlight and looked out at the night. And it wishes.

Then one more family comes.
The house tries not to hope.
But something makes it hold its breath.

There are children. And they're saying, "This one!
This one! Please, can we live here? Please?"
No one answers No or Yes, but the house is sure
it hears the mother say, "It almost feels we
were expected."

In the meadow, dandelions wait to be wished on.
And the family seems to know.
They each bend down to pick a stem.
Are they wishing what the house is wishing?
It is certain they are its family—

until they go away.

That night the stars and the moon are small comfort.
And it is the same the next night. And the next.

Then? The house barely dares to believe what it sees.
The family is back! They are back to stay.

They fix what needs fixing and paint what needs painting.
But they don't talk of changing things or Adding Onto.

They look out the windows at what the house has looked at.

They listen to what it's listened to for so many years.

They take time to notice and to wonder.

They find the swing in the tree.

They want to know what the house can
tell them about Long Ago and Used to Be.

But that's not all.

For now the family and the house wake
every morning to what a new day brings—

for making new memories, together.